She Could Not

Help Herself

By

Stiletto Desires

Welcome you saucy purveyors of sultriness. I am Stiletto Desires, your host and bringer of steamy tales with which to whet your fantasies and longing hungers. Contained within these pages are confessions of naughtiness told only in hushed tones and behind closed doors in intimate company. Know that these stories were given freely and anonymously. Because of that some details were omitted and others changed in order to keep things anonymous. But you must be thinking the same questions I did.

Are they real?

Did they actually occur?

Honestly I do not care as it does not matter. They fired something deep when I heard them just as they will with you.

Do you dare continue?

Are you wishing to ignite your imagination and possibly other things?

Will you chance exploring the landscape of heated desire as it fuels your own?

Of course you do. So grab a glass of wine, or whatever your poison is, sit down and get comfortable. And when you are ready for some passion and ecstasy turn the page and read on.

Just remember I bear no responsibility for any desires and fantasies you create or enact as a result of these stories. That's all on you sirens of sexiness. Don't worry, I don't judge now enjoy and indulge.

Love in Crisis

Dear Stiletto Desires,

I can't believe I'm writing this but I felt I had to tell someone. You see I've been married for almost ten years but lately its felt more like twenty. I don't know what happened or what had gone wrong. I suppose like most I was worried that I was falling out of love with my husband and that our marriage was coming to an end. But I suppose I should talk about why I felt this way.

I've heard the stories of how other couples fall out of love and simply divorce. I've had this happen to a couple of friends but I never thought it would happen to me. That is such a cliché thing to say I realize but it's true. See when we first were married we could not keep our hands off each other. The kitchen, our bedroom, in the shower, hell even once it was the backseat of our car like we were teenagers again.

But sadly as time went on and our lives progressed we found ourselves becoming busier and busier with our jobs. We started to put off our love making here and there. It was only one time we'd tell ourselves though in truth we were simply trying to convince ourselves this decision was not one we secretly hated. It was easy you know? By the time we got home we were both tired and just not in the mood. And it became routine and soon it became our new life together.

It's not like we stopped our love making cold turkey, we still had sex. The problem is we ended up having it only on our anniversary and Christmas and other holidays. If we wanted to get passionate any other time we had to schedule it. I can't tell you how cold and mechanical that felt especially on the times we were just tired and not able to perform like we used to.

God how I missed my husband and the touch he used to have. But he's not to blame, he didn't rob me of my passion or our love making. No, it was our chosen life path. We talked about it and we agreed we'd work hard to achieve our goals and build up a nest egg. Then take it easy and just be with each other, maybe plan a family finally. At least that was the plan and one I thought would work.

Unfortunately as we worked and worked saving and scrimping as much as we could I felt what passion I had left slowly dying. And I wasn't alone in that. I could see it in my husband's eyes. The way he looked at me now was not how he looked at me when we first got married. The fiery passion that would ignite in those beautiful brown eyes of his when he saw me bend over or wear something sexy just did not appear anymore even when I wore his favorite outfit.

It was heartbreaking to say the least. I no longer felt desired by my husband. Oh it'd be easy to blame him but that'd be cowardly and irresponsible. I'm just as much to blame adding guilt to my loss of passion and the combination made me feel desperate and scared. I began to wonder that even if we did build up that nest egg would it be too late? Would my husband still want me? Would I still want him?

I needed to know if I was still a creature to be desired but my husband was always at work now. Too busy working himself to death to build that goddamn nest egg I was now beginning to hate. So in desperation I made a decision, an impulsive one I hoped I would not regret. I ran out and bought an outfit, a slutty one, far sluttier than I normally would wear. Not like a hooker, I wasn't that desperate, but a leather miniskirt with a bustier and lace. It was totally not me but I had to know if I was still desirable. Besides it covered everything tastefully, well as tastefully as such an outfit can be, but showed enough cleavage and skin to make me enticing, or so I hoped. I kept up with my yoga so the outfit would show off how shapely I was. All I needed was the courage because I only wanted to tempt other men not take them home.

It took a few days of talking to myself in the mirror to finally convince myself to just up and do it. Things were getting worse and I really needed to know. Because if the spark was truly gone then maybe our love wasn't far behind if it already hadn't faded away.

So one night when I knew my husband was going to be late again I squeezed into the outfit, my boobs were pushed more out than I would've liked but then that's why I bought this thing. Then I put on my make-up, making sure to remember what my mom always told me that make-up was meant to accentuate what I had and not replace it. Then when I finished getting my hair to match the sexiness I was hoping to feel I paused to look at myself in the mirror and judge.

I'd be lying if I said I didn't feel scared but after seeing myself in the mirror I knew I was as hot as I was going to be. I only hoped that if I succeeded any man wanting me would take rejection well or that I would not give in and cheat on my husband. So I put on my stilettos and got in my car then drove off to a classy bar my husband talked about taking me to once we had our nest egg. Maybe I shouldn't have, especially with how I was dressed, but he made it sound so nice and elegant how could I resist?

Once I got there it was certainly classy as there they had a valet to park my car. I'll admit I was a bit disappointed the bouncer didn't ask for my ID but then I wasn't twenty anymore and it's just sad when a woman can't accept that. But I entered and was awed, my husband was right this place was classy. The room was just the right shade of darkness. Enough to give the illusion of privacy but not so dark as to make it difficult to make out anything. There were lovely paintings, not the gaudy prints like you find in a hotel, but I imagine by an actual artist who had an arrangement with the bar to help sell their art. The walls were white with gold painted trim, it felt rather gauche but I saw what the owners were going for.

There were plenty of booths which I was tempted to sit in but since I was here to be seen I instead sat at the bar, ordered a white wine and waited. I did my best to pretend to not be looking like was hoping for attention. I had no idea if I was or not but I suspected my lack of acting experience betrayed my intent. To help with this I got on my phone and looked at what was on social media, see what my friends were up to. I felt bad about not inviting them but this had to be secret, nobody could know or else it could be misconstrued into something marriage ending.

So there I waited, sipping my wine, and ordering a second glass when the first one ended, and swiping at my phone in an obvious attempt to be seen. As I thought about it I began to feel embarrassed. In the time I was there not one man came up to me, hell not even one lesbian. It started to build up in me and I began to feel a fool. I wondered then if maybe I had gone too far, that maybe I looked as desperate as I had felt when I bought this outfit. God, how stupid I felt then.

But then a smell of cologne, the type my husband used to wear, graced my nose. It distracted me from my lowering self-esteem and thank God for that. I wanted to turn and look at my unintentional savior but remembered why I was sitting at that bar in the first place and simply pretended I did not care he was there.

"It's never good to drink alone, especially for one as beautiful as you," the stranger enticed.

I have to say as bold as this man was it felt good, far better than I expected and if I was in my right mind I would've realized how dangerous that was to my marriage. But I wasn't in my right mind and wanted to see just how much he desired me. Was he here thinking I was an easy fuck? Or did he genuinely believe I was beautiful? I had to know.

"Maybe I want to be alone," I replied hoping he'd realize I was playing his game.

"Do you?" he asked.

I smiled, he was good at this. It still didn't answer my question but to be flirted with like this, it had been a long time. It was a nectar I never knew I needed until that moment.

"I may be accepting of some company but only if the company is a respectful one," I accepted.

"Of course, a woman of such obvious refined tastes deserves respect. Shall I have the bartender freshen your wine?" he asked.

Maybe I shouldn't have let him sit with me. He did after all approach me and compliment me and in hindsight that was the validation I was looking for. But the way he smelled, the way he talked, I didn't want it to end, not yet anyway. I had missed such attentions from my husband and it felt so good finally getting them again. No, I needed this, I deserved this.

"Sure," I simply said.

I then finally turned to look at him, this stranger, and was taken aback by how beautiful he was. Even though he was clean shaved he had a ruggedness that clung him handsomely. His hair was thinning but still well-kept and styled. His eyes though, they were just like my husband's, brown and beautiful and easy to fall into.

"Do you often walk into a bar alone to pick up strange women?" I asked after he had ordered two wines from the bartender.

I cringed inside. I couldn't believe I had said that but it had been so long and did not know what else to say. But he simply smiled, a boyishly charming one it turned out to be.

"No, normally I wouldn't approach so lovely a customer of my bar but when I saw you I knew I had to come talk to you," he admitted.

Now I smiled. The owner? Did he really expect me to believe that? But then it did prove he was really trying to get with me. I admit I felt myself moisten and if I wasn't so invested in this I would've heard that part of my brain screaming at me reminding me I was married. Instead I wanted to see just how far he was willing to go.

"The owner huh? Then how about you get us the best bottle in the house and we go find ourselves a booth?" I challenged.

I knew in this place such a bottle would cost far more than most could afford but if he was really wanting me as badly as he seemed he would buy that bottle. His smile never wavered as he then turned to the bartender and ordered a bottle of wine. I had no idea if it was the best the place had to offer but I did know it was an expensive wine, several hundred at least, maybe a thousand bucks. I couldn't believe it and I could myself starting to heat up from lust and my pussy getting wetter. I should've ended it there and then, I should've told him I was married and walked out but I didn't and I don't know why.

Instead I found myself walking with him and our expensive wine to a booth. We beside each other on one side, it probably looked ridiculous both of us sitting on one side but honestly I wanted him to sit next to me. I wanted to feel the heat from his body and drink in his cologne and be close enough to imagine his chest and what it looked like without his shirt on. That scared me and it broke me out of my growing lust. I tried to cool my pussy as it was beginning to ache and I did not want to betray my husband. But then would it be a betrayal if our marriage was already dead?

The stranger poured the wine and I sipped. It was exquisite. I never thought to ever taste such an intoxicating drink and combined with the wine I already had drank that evening I could feel myself losing control.

"So how is it?" the stranger asked.

"Excellent, you have great taste in wine," I complimented.

"Thank you but I imagine it doesn't taste as good as you," he replied.

My heart raced and I felt myself getting even warmer and start to tingle. Normally I would've said something harsh or slapped him or thrown the wine in his face but I didn't. Instead I put my hand on his thigh and started imagining him tasting me all over, being on me and being in me. I wanted him, badly, and I should've left. But I smiled, took another sip and moved my hand up his thigh and to his crotch. I could feel his dick and it was hard and throbbing.

He smiled in return and he then leaned in close and softly kissed me. He then placed his hand on thigh and it was then I realized I had subconsciously spread my legs slightly. I couldn't believe how much I wanted this man and I wanted him to have me. I kissed him back as his hand slid slowly up to my pussy. I unzipped his pants and slid my hand into them so I could grab his member and start massaging it. He gave a soft moan that he tried to stifle so no one would hear. He slipped his hand under my panties and started to rub my clit and tease my hole by dipping a tip of finger in then remove it. It drove me wild, I needed him and I was going to have him. I knew he felt the same. My bustier felt so restricting then and I needed it off and him on my tits but where we could do this?

"As the owner you should know of a place more private for us to go," I softly said in my best sexy voice.

"No place that would attract attention from the staff. We'll have to make do with the bathrooms," the stranger offered.

I would've scoffed if I wasn't so turned on and lusting so much. It is such a cliché but in a place like this the real owner likely would've ensured the staff kept the bathrooms clean and sanitized.

"The women's, don't keep me waiting," I ordered.

I replaced his hard cock back into his pants and rezipped him, being careful to ensure nothing unfortunate happened to it. He then grabbed my panties and slid them off. It was so bold and risky it turned me on even more. God I swear I would've jumped him there and then if I had the courage to do so. After he freed my pussy I took another sip of the wine, kissed him again then headed to the bathroom. As soon as I got in I bent low to see if anyone else was there in the stalls.

Thankfully I saw no feet and sighed in relief. Last thing I wanted was for someone to overhear. But then I realized I didn't care and honestly it was kinda hot knowing I was so desirable that someone could get off hearing me fuck some stranger in the bathroom. With a grin I could not get rid of I took a moment to look at myself in the mirror. What looked back was a smiling goddess and my husband suddenly was forgotten.

The stranger then came in and practically ran up to me and wrapped his arms around me. Immediately one hand slid down to my ass where he squeezed it and pressed me hard against him. I gasped when I could and he followed it up by having his other hand feel my tits over my bustier. I held him tight and pressed him as hard against me as I could. I then maneuvered him to the nearest stall, rather clumsily as we banged into the side of it.

But we didn't care, we kissed and I immediately went for his pants. He turned me around and let go of me so he could close and lock the stall door. Once he turned back around I was already on my knees grabbing his pants and unzipping them. His hard cock was soon out and in my mouth. He grunted as I sucked and twisted his shaft. I only hoped he wouldn't cum in my mouth as there was far more I was going to do with him before we finished. But it was then I got a mouthful as he shot his load into my mouth.

"Sorry, it's just that you're so beautiful. But keep going, I got more," he offered breathily so lost in lust he was.

I swallowed his cream and stroked his dick to keep it hard just in case. I stood up and he grabbed me and roughly turned me around then bent me over. I couldn't help but moan a little but that would pale in comparison when he lifted my skirt and rammed his cock into my now dripping pussy.

"Yes!" I loosed.

Again and again he pulled almost all the way out only to stop and ram himself all the way back in. It felt so good and my pussy was really missing this. I didn't want him to stop and if he came inside me I didn't care, I just wanted him that badly. He grunted with every thrust and I screamed with every pounding. But just as I was getting more and more into it he stopped and pulled out. I stood up and looked at him angrily, I wasn't finished and I wanted his cock. But I misunderstood, he grabbed me and kissed me hard all the while reaching behind me to undo my bustier. Once he did then moved me to the door of the stall and tore of my top and went down on my tits.

I moaned and grabbed his head. I closed my eyes and looked to the ceiling as he sucked my nipples pausing to flick them with his tongue. First one, then the other then he stood upright and I opened my eyes to look at him. He paused to kiss me once more then grabbed me by my legs, lifted me up, legs spread, then rammed his cock in me again. I screamed but did not close my eyes and neither did he. We grunted and continued to stare as he rammed harder and faster. He was going to cum again and I couldn't wait for it to shoot into me.

"Yes! Yes!" I found myself loosing as he thrusted.

He grunted with every push and he got even faster and faster and I could feel he was about to cum again. I kissed him one last time before he arched back and came. He must've shot a lot because his sex face did not drop for some time. Once he was done I wrapped my legs tight around him because I wanted to keep his cock in me just a little longer. It had felt so good and I just wanted a little more. He did not resist and wrapped his arms around me and kissed me. He then stared into my eyes and smiled.

"God you are so beautiful and I don't even know your name," he confessed.

I smiled in return. This was exactly what I had been wanting all along and it was then I remembered why I was here in the first place. Suddenly I remembered my husband but oddly I felt no guilt. In truth I did not want any kind of relationship with this handsome stranger. I just wanted to be desired, to be held and treated as my husband used to and this stranger gave me exactly what I needed. I then got off his cock and looked at him straight in the eyes, those beautiful brown eyes of his.

"I don't know yours either and I don't want to. Maybe we'll run into each other again in another bar or maybe we won't. Either way this is all it was," I said.

He looked a little disappointed but he nodded. He put away his now flaccid dick and adjusted his clothes to be more presentable. He then moved me to the side so he could get out of the stall but before he did he reached up and caressed my face with his hand, smiled then turned around and left. I'll admit that gesture got my heart fluttering because it was something my husband used to do.

I cleaned myself up and dressed. I could still taste his cock and his cum and I hoped my husband was too tired to want to do anything when I got home, assuming he would be home when I got back. I checked myself out in the mirror to ensure my make-up was okay, and fixed what I could, then left the bar and went back home.

When I pulled up back in the driveway I saw my husband had actually gotten home and I wondered if he was staying awake to wait for me. I paused to consider what I would say to him when I saw him. Once I decided I got out and walked into our house. As soon as I was in I took off my stilettos, thankful because they're really not comfortable, then walked into the living room where my husband was watching TV.

"Quite an outfit honey," he greeted when he saw me.

"I just wanted to feel desirable. You were late coming to the bar. That was my second glass of wine when you finally approached me. What happened?" I asked as I joined him on the couch.

"Sorry about that. My boss called and I had to diplomatically tell him no. Took a while because he decided to be an asshole about it. But I wasn't about to disappoint my wife on our first role-playing night," he informed me.

"So you liked it?" I purred.

There was that boyishly charming grin of his again.

"Of course, you did make me cum twice," he said.

I smiled in return and wrapped my arms around him and held him tight. That's right Stiletto Desires, this was all a role-play me and my husband cooked up to save our marriage. And saved it it did. The passion came back and we're back to being on each other like horny teenagers. I haven't felt this fulfilled and wanted in a long time.

Back when we talked about our marriage, when I feared it was collapsing, he confessed he felt the same and he too feared our marriage was ending. But we both came to realize it was because we were so focused on our goals and so focused on the future we left no time for ourselves or the present. It was a hard lesson to learn but an extremely fun one I will never forget.

Thank you for reading this Stiletto Desires, I hope my crisis can help you and whoever you share it with.

Love in Crisis

Well Miss Love in Crisis, I can say your story has helped me on cold and lonely nights but whether it will for my readers only they can say. So does it you lovely sirens? No need to answer, I think we already know.

So how did that live up to your expectations?

Did you see the twist coming?

Are you ready for more?

Maybe you should take a break, maybe you need some cool down time. Or maybe you need a role-playing night of your own before continuing. Or maybe you're insatiable and need what's next.

Whatever you decide, whenever you're ready our next confessor will be waiting with all the dirty details you can handle.

First Time

Dear Stiletto Desires,

I don't really know what to write because I mean it seems so lame. But then again this is all anonymous right? You say you don't judge and I'm going to hold you to that. I suppose I should just tell you my story. I'll be honest it feels a little embarrassing to do this but I haven't told anyone because of fear it would get back to my father. But I really do need to tell someone.

Okay let me start by saying I'm not a teenager, just a barely in her twenties who still lives with her dad. Lame right? But I mean where else can I go? Things are shit out there and I'm not about to work at some fast food place but whatever, I'm supposed to be writing about a sexy time right? Sorry about that, I'll try to be adult about all this.

So yea, my parents are well to do which means I have everything I could possibly want. I'll be honest I feel bad about whining about my parents because they do love me and shit and could just kick me out. But okay, this is harder than I thought. Alright serious time, anyway we have a pool and we have some guys come from time to time to clean it and do our yard and stuff. Sometimes they get some really hot guys doing it and as much as I love watching them take their shirts off I always stayed away. I never knew what my parents would do, especially my dad. He's rather protective of me even though I'm an adult.

Anyway just this last summer the guys came over and there was one who was seriously hot. You could see his muscles through his shirt and he always had that stubble that's just sexy. Would it be too much to say I got wet every time I saw him? My room overlooks the pool so I would peak through the curtains to watch him especially when he took his shirt off on the really hot days. I think he noticed me watching him but I suppose it wasn't much of a secret.

There were times when he would take off his shirt then glance in the direction of my room. It scared me but also excited me. I mean he really wanted me and it started to infect my dreams. I'd wake up needing my panties changed because of how hot my dreams would be. So I would watch him from my window and imagine what it would be like to be in his arms and my legs wrapped around his waist.

As the days went by it really got to me. I'd get so wet and I'd ache so badly that while I'd watch I found myself sliding my own panties down and start rubbing my clit. I'd grab my own breast and squeeze imagining it was him touching me and wishing he would do things with his tongue to me. I'd rub harder and faster until I could stand it no more and rushed to my bed where I would strip naked and lie down.

I reached to my pussy and shoved two fingers inside. I moaned as I imagined it was his hard dick inside me and not my fingers. I grabbed one of my breasts and squeezed it also imagining it was him doing the squeezing. I could feel my toes curl as I shoved my fingers in and out faster and faster. All the while I would moan with each thrust of my fingers. Fearing I would attract the attention of my parents I grabbed my pillow and roughly shoved it into my mouth. I bit down hard on it as I continued to force my fingers in and out of my aching wet pussy. I couldn't believe how hot it got from just imagining this guy fucking me, imagine if he actually was.

I grabbed my other breast and pinched my nipple forcing me to moan into my pillow. I couldn't stand it I needed to rub my clit so I pulled out my fingers and rubbed and spanked it. I imagined him between my thighs ramming me again and again. So

I rubbed again and again, it wasn't enough I needed my fingers back inside so I shoved them in and fucked my pussy as hard as I could. Then finally when I imagined he had cum did I stop and pulled out my fingers.

I laid there breathing heavily. It wasn't the first time I masturbated but it was the first time I did it that hard to myself. Something was different about it though and at the time I was not sure what that was. I couldn't believe how much of a mess I made but that's okay, ever since I started masturbating I always made sure I washed my own sheets. Really don't need my parents knowing anything you know? But if this sounds like the end of my story, just wait because it isn't. This is all just for context.

Well this became something of a routine for me. As the summer days went by and he would show up I'd hide away and watch him then touch myself. A lot of times I ended up losing interest with other guys who I'd masturbate to. But not this guy, I don't know what it was about him but I never lost interest. In fact I just wanted him more each time I touched myself to him. Thinking about it that's probably how it happened.

You see the end of the summer finally started to come and it would soon be the last time my dad would have the guys come. This meant I probably would never see this guy again. Which honestly I was kinda glad for because there were times I fucked my pussy so hard I was sore for a whole day. I mean a dude doing it to you like that is one thing, doing it to yourself is another.

So anyway it was one of the last days he would be coming by to clean our pool and do our yard. I looked out the window, hiding behind the curtains, and he noticed because he glanced right at me and took his shirt off. He smiled and then continued his work. Like most days there was only one guy who would clean the pool and the others would take care of the front and back yard. Because of this I knew the guy would be there by himself for however long it took him to clean the pool. That's when I got the idea.

It was crazy and I couldn't believe I even thought of it. I mean what if someone saw? What if my parents or even just my dad? I knew I shouldn't do it but then I felt I had to. This pool guy gave me a lot of pleasure just showing off it seemed only fair to do the same. So taking a deep breath I stripped naked then flung my curtains open. I stood there totally nude and looking down at him. He looked up and raised his eyebrows in shock. I noticed his cock was hard and I bet it was throbbing inside of those shorts of his.

I smiled then slowly turned around letting him drink in all of me. I could see he was struggling to control himself. I knew he wanted to run into my house and throw me onto my bed and fuck my brains out. But I also knew my parents were home and that's what was stopping him. That knowledge only made me hotter and wetter. I could see his hand was twitching and I couldn't help but giggle. Since he was denied my pussy he wanted to whip it out and yank it for me. I wish he did to be honest, I would have loved to have seen that dick of his and his sex face as he shot out his load into our pool.

But I suppose that was kinda cruel so instead I started to touch myself. I kept my eyes on him the entire time as I masturbated for him. I first grabbed my breasts with both hands and slowly worked them. My nipples grew erect and sensitive and I could feel my pussy juices start to drip down my legs. I shifted my stance slightly to spread my legs and he looked never once blinking.

I'll admit it was intoxicating knowing he wanted me so much he was willing to risk having my parents walk out into the pool area and see his raging hard-on. I then squeezed my tits when he looked back up and brought one up so I could suck on my own nipple. He licked his lips when I did and I couldn't help but smile. I then let go of one of my breasts and slid my hand slowly down my body, past my stomach and then finally to my pussy. I gave it a soft pat to get some of my juices on my fingers then pulled my hand away. I turned my hand towards him so he could see the wetness now on my fingers. He quickly looked around, probably to see if anyone was looking, then looked back and his mouth was slightly open. I could see his dick was throbbing obviously and it must've been torture for him to be so denied me and my pussy. But I wasn't done, not by a long shot.

Keeping my eyes on him I brought my hand to my mouth and inserted my fingers so I could suck my own juices off of them. His reaction was restrained but I saw his dick throb yet again. Man he must've been worried he'd cream his shorts right then and there. Once I had cleaned my fingers of my wetness I brought them back to my tits and squeezed them. I lifted one to my mouth again and then sucked my nipple again. I then pulled out my nipple and paused to look at him and his restrained desire. I smiled then brought my other nipple to my mouth where I gently bit it before sucking. I could see he was imagining himself doing it as his mouth moved along with mine.

This was making me so wet and ache so bad that I needed my pussy touched and entered. I spread my legs a little more and brought my hand down to start rubbing my clit. I then shoved two of my fingers into me and slowly pulled them out. I then pushed them back in and squeezed my tit with my other hand as I did so. I could see he was starting to breath heavy and I wondered if I could get him to cum in his shorts. I thought since I had come this far I might as well go all in.

I then let go of my breast and pressed myself up against my window. The glass was cold but I barely noticed. Having my tits and nipples squished up against it I imagined would be like squishing them against his smooth muscled pecs. With my own sex face on I started to ram my pussy with my fingers harder than before. I slowly started to build up speed as a shoved my fingers as far in as I could then pulled them almost all the way out. I intentionally would tap the glass so my juices would get on it and he could see just how wet I was, how wet he was making me. At last he couldn't stop himself and his hand found its way to his cock. He did not shove his hand into his shorts, he left it outside to massage his dick from the outside. I suppose he can't be blamed, he was making me fuck myself after all.

Faster and faster I rammed my fingers in and out and each time I would moan. Realizing my parents might hear me as my moans were getting louder with each thrust I grabbed my curtains with my free hand and shoved them into my mouth. It was a good thing too because soon my moans were becoming screams. I then shifted my hand so whenever I pulled out my fingers I'd rub my clit doing so. It was something I loved doing since it often made me tingle and sent shivers through me.

I rubbed and rubbed staring at him as he stared at me. He massaged himself more blatantly and I could see he how tortured he was being forced to stand there and not actually touch me. His hips started to quiver as did mine. We wanted each other, we were masturbating for each other and my fingers worked harder and faster the longer this went on. I had no doubt he was ready to pop and something inside me was building and I didn't know what.

"Honey? I'm going to go get us some dinner. You alright with burgers?" my dad called loudly from behind my bedroom door.

I was so thankful I had thought to shove the curtains into my mouth because hearing my dad suddenly talk to me from nowhere made me scream. But it also did something else. Suddenly I was shaking and pussy was spasming. It wasn't until after that all stopped when I saw I had sprayed all over the window. I quickly looked over my shoulder, spit out my curtains then doing my best to sound normal I shouted back to my dad.

"Yea that's fine dad, make sure to get the fries and a chocolate shake okay?" I said.

I suppose that was stupid to say but I really didn't want him thinking something was up and come in and see me naked and masturbating.

"Of course honey, I'll let you know when I get back. You've got a good view of the pool. Are the guys working? Are they doing a good job?" my dad called back.

I pulled out my fingers and looked over to the pool guy. I could see a wet stain on the front of his shorts. I muffled my giggle as I realized he came in his shorts just as I was hoping I'd get him to.

"Yea, he did a real good job dad, really good," I said though I wasn't referring to the pool.

"Good, glad to hear that. Alright I'm out, I'll be back pumpkin," my dad said

"Later dad," I called back.

I gave the pool guy one last smile then licked and kissed the glass. He smiled and shook his head then went back to work. I closed my curtains and made a mental note to clean my window before my parents could see the mess I made on it.

But that's my story Stiletto Desires, it was the first time I ever experienced an orgasm. I never once thought it'd be like that. I kinda wish it was that pool guy who gave me it. But then again he might get ideas about us or my dad might so it was best things worked out this way. I never did see him again after that, I'm still not sure if that's a good thing or not.

So um, I guess that's it. I don't know how to end this so I guess I'll just do it. Thanks for listening or reading or whatever, you know what I mean.

First Time

Oh no worries Miss First Time, I mean it when I say I don't judge and I certainly won't judge how you came to have your first orgasm. But maybe it helped some of my sultry sirens reading this to have one of their own. I have to say though Miss First Time you getting that man to cream his own shorts without even touching him? That's a little impressive, maybe in time you can teach us all a thing or two. There is something you should consider though. If you think about it in a way he did give you that orgasm. So don't be disheartened, instead embrace it for what it was, an exciting experience that was both wonderful and naughty. What more could a girl want?

So dear sirens what do you think?

Did this remind you of your first orgasm?

How was it?

Or have you not had one yet?

Shall I continue so you do?

Of course you want me to continue, you didn't get this book just for one or two vicarious experiences. Oh no, you want it all and all you shall have because we all have needs and I aim to feed them. So when you are ready read on and see what's next.

Insatiable

Dear Stiletto Desires,

I can't believe I'm writing this to you because honestly it seems weird. But also it seems kinda liberating to spill my sexual secrets and I'll admit if it helps others get off that's actually kinda hot. I've never been what you would call a one man kinda gal. What can I say? I like cock and I like men, all kinds of men. I like the shaved ones, the hairy ones, tall, short, big penis, average penis, even the scrawny or fat ones can have moves that can surprise a girl. It's a smorgasbord of man meat out there and I just love sampling it all. Yea, it's kinda stupid but a girl has needs so fuck it and fuck any who disapprove.

I did try getting serious and sticking with a single guy once and I suppose that'll be the story I tell you. This happened years ago after I left college and was just starting my career, you'll understand if I don't reveal that I hope. This is all supposed to be anonymous as you say. But anyway at that time in my life I thought I was of the age to stop sleeping around and get serious with my life. Heh, little did I know.

So I met a guy through my job, a former client of the company who moved on, and we hit it off. He wasn't all that good looking really but he was respectful and never was an asshole to me. I don't mean he was a pushover pussy type but someone who got me and was nice even when he stood up to me when I needed to be. Not a lot of guys are like that, he's the type you want to stay with. Maybe it was the wrong reason to be with him but like I said I thought it was time I started being mature.

Things were well enough between us. I actually did come to have deep feelings for him but I'm not sure if I loved him. They say if you don't know if you're in love then you probably aren't. That sounds like bullshit to me but not like I'm an expert. But the biggest problem with our relationship was the sex lacked passion. I mean it was fine and fed my needs but it was like eating a fruit salad when I really wanted a bacon cheeseburger. I considered leaving him over that but when I thought about it I realized I was just being selfish so I stayed with him. Still those feelings of lack of fulfillment persisted and I began to feel trapped.

Well one day he had an old college buddy come over to visit us and this guy was not too bad looking. He wasn't like those Hollywood hunks but handsome enough I imagine he never had women issues. I think he would've been a lot hotter had he exercised. Muscles do wonders for a man's sexiness not to mention the added bedroom benefits. But still, attractive nonetheless and I've fucked uglier so who was I to judge?

At any rate when my boyfriend introduced me to him I could see it in his friend's eyes he wanted me. I know that totally sounds narcissistic but I swear it was true. I didn't say anything of course, that would only cause all sorts of needless bullshit. So we all spent the night together hanging out, watching movies and listening to my boyfriend and his friend reminisce and tell me funny stories of when they were younger.

Turns out his friend was in town for a week or so on business and thought he'd use that as an opportunity to catch up. So as the days went on we spent more and more time together. Each time it was the same but with each visit his friend kept eyeing me more. I could see him checking out my tits when my boyfriend wasn't looking and if I hadn't got off on that I would've said something. I told you I love men and old habits die hard.

Well on his last day in town his friend showed up but of course my boyfriend was at work and would be for hours. I invited him in not because I liked his company, turns out he's a bit of a ponce, but he was on the attractive side and I liked how he looked at me. But turns out he had plans of his own and he was more of a ponce than I thought.

You see after I invited him in and he sat down I offered to get us both beers. He accepted and I went into the kitchen to get them. After I pulled out two bottles from the fridge I turned around and he was standing there watching me and I could see the crotch of his pants were bulging. I'll admit I got a little wet from this. But I also knew for certain why he was here now.

"Look, you're a good looking guy but I'm dating your friend. So just leave okay?" I told him.

"Yet you're looking at me like I'm looking at you. You saw how hard my dick is and yet you're not upset. I don't think you want me to leave," he countered.

In most situations I would've kicked him in the crotch and got out of there, phone the cops and all that. But he was right, I didn't want him to leave because he was chock full of the passion I've been missing. But I wasn't going to give it up that easily.

"Right because asking you to leave is too subtle for you to understand?" I shot back.

I placed the beers on the counter next to me and stood there standing my ground. I could feel myself getting aroused, I had missed the passion more than I thought. He walked towards me then stopped right in front of me. His smell was intoxicating. He looked deep into my eyes and I could feel his bulge touch me and it excited me.

"Not at all, I can see it in your eyes and the fact you aren't pushing me away or trying to leave or even getting angry has me wondering. I think you want me as much as I want you. But I won't force anything, only a pussy does that. A real man gets invited and that's all you have to do, invite me to touch you, lick you, please you," he challenged.

I had to take a moment to compose myself. This was a lot to take in after so long of no passion. I hoped he couldn't tell that I was practically dripping right now.

"And if I don't?" I asked.

That seemed stupid, it's practically an invitation but I suppose that's what I was doing because it was what I wanted I knew.

"Then I leave but I do have an argument you may not be able to counter," he said.

Before I could ask what that argument was he leaned in and kissed me. It was a good kiss, his pushed his tongue into my mouth and I reciprocated. We rolled our tongues around each other, massaging each other and next thing I knew my arms were wrapped around him holding him against me. His hands found their way to my ass and he grabbed and squeezed hard. That stopped our kiss as I gasped and we paused to look at each other. It was stupid to deny this anymore, he was right I wanted him as much as he wanted me so I caved and kissed him again.

As we kissed he moved one of his hands up my body to my shirt where he roughly grabbed my tit over my shirt. I moaned a little which seemed to excite him further as with his other hand he let go of my ass only to slap it. I grunted, pulled back to slap him, it was just too early for that kind of stuff. He grabbed my wrist and roughly twisted it behind my back and I kissed him in response. He kissed me back then let go of me altogether so he grab my jeans and start undoing them. I did the same, I grabbed at his belt buckle and undid it then I undid his jeans and opened his pants. I greedily reached in to grab his hard cock which throbbed in my hand when I grabbed it.

As I did so he grabbed at my shirt and tore it open. My shirt buttons exploded everywhere and he yanked if off me. I started to yank on his dick and grabbed my bra from the front and pulled it upwards freeing my breasts. It kinda hurt a little but I didn't care, I was horny as hell and just wanted him to taste me and fuck me. And taste me he did because once my tits were out he bent down and started sucking on them. While he was sucking and nibbling on one of my tits he reached up with one hand and squeezed the other. He pinched that nipple which forced me to gasp and moan.

With his other hand he reached down and shoved my panties and jeans down as far as he could. He then roughly shoved his hand between my legs and shoved his fingers into my pussy. I moaned again and wished he would just ram his cock in but I think he just wanted to make this last as long as he could. Not that I blame him, I'm always happy to fuck a guy for as long as he can handle it. He pulled his fingers out then pinched my clit and that made me scream. I was not expecting that and it caused me to yank hard on his cock which I had not let go of. He grunted then pulled back and paused to look at me.

We shared a moment before he bent down, spread my legs then placed his mouth on my pussy so he could massage my clit with his tongue. I grabbed his head and held it against me and hoped he would he shove his tongue into my aching pussy. I would not be disappointed. After he massaged my clit for a bit he pulled back and gently bit it. I moaned yet again and he then shoved his mouth on my pussy again but this time he shoved his tongue into me.

It was wild as he would wiggle his tongue hitting me inside in just the right spot. I moaned louder and hoped he would last. But it turns out he couldn't. After he wiggled his tongue inside tasting all he could he then pulled out his tongue and suck on my pussy lips for a second. Then he stood up and roughly turned me around and pushed me against my kitchen counter. I was a little angry actually because I wanted him to get on his back so I could get on top and grind his dick off. But he seemed a bit angry himself as once I was up against the counter bent over exposing my pussy in full he grabbed hips and rammed as hard as he could into my pussy.

I screamed from how good it felt and he pulled out and rammed hard again. Again and again he rammed and I screamed each time. He then let go of my hips and grabbed my hair and yanked back on it hard. I screamed from the pain but it seemed to excite him more since he only rammed faster and faster. His grunting was becoming louder and starting to become screams themselves. He then he rammed me one last time and stopped then screamed. He was cumming and that kinda pissed me off because I wanted to see his sex face.

Once he finished screaming he paused to slap my ass hard then he pulled out and I could feel his jizz oozing down my leg. What he didn't know though was the anger I was feeling was still there and it deepened because while he was finished I wasn't. And I was not about to be denied, not after all this. I turned around quick and I could see that dumb smile all guys have after they cum. I quickly hooked my leg behind his then pushed against him as hard as I could. His smiled disappeared when he fell over hard onto his back.

"What the fuck?" he exclaimed.

But I didn't answer, instead I jumped on him and grabbed his cock then started massaging and yanking to get it hard again. And it responded. He grunted and his face contortioned into pain, his member was highly sensitive and I smiled at that thought, I wanted him to get as angry I was since it would make the sex all that much better. Once his dick was hard again I tore off my jeans as quickly as I could. He tried to get up but I kicked him in his chest and kept my foot on it to keep him pinned to the floor.

"It's my turn, I'm not done," I told him.

I could see the confusion on his face. I'm betting he never had a woman dominate him like this before. It figures from the way he fucks he's used to being the dominant one but he was about to learn a hard and very fun lesson. I then dropped and grabbed his cock again. I shoved it into my mouth and started sucking. I grabbed his shaft and started twisting and he moaned in response. I would've tickled his balls but really I wanted to have my way and finish this up. After sucking on him for a bit I could see he was getting close to cumming again so I stopped, stood up then straddled him. He tried to get up again but I kicked his chest again and shoved him back down.

I then lowered myself and guided his throbbing cock to my pussy then sat on it. I started to grind and bent down to help do that. He took the opportunity to suck on my tits again and I moaned and luxuriated in that. He grabbed my hips and helped guide them so I would grind his dick in the way he wanted. His moans grew louder and louder and I straightened up so his dick was fully in me and I could just grind it while it was fully inside.

"Yes," I moaned.

Finally he could stand no more and he quickly sat up and grabbed me to stop me. He screamed as he came again and I wrapped my arms around him holding him tight against me. Once he was done shooting his second load he collapsed onto the floor but I stayed on him and laid down with him. We kissed but I kept slowly grinding, I just wanted a little more and didn't want to get off him yet.

"Wow, I didn't think you were the type to be on top," he stupidly commented.

Why some guys need to say something stupid after they fuck is beyond me. But I sat up and slapped his face really hard then stood up and started gathering my clothes.

"What the fuck? What was that for?" he asked.

He sounded pretty freaked so I suppose I had to explain.

"Because you're stupid. We fucked betraying my boyfriend and your friend. We were horny but we could've resisted but you couldn't and didn't," I told him as I put on my panties getting it soaked with a mixture of my juices and his jizz.

"Hey it takes two to tango you know," he angrily rebutted.

"Yea exactly, because I was horny too and I couldn't resist when you couldn't. So get dressed then take your bruised ego and fuck off. Don't ever come back," I chastised him.

I felt like such a mom saying that to him but he needed to be treated like a child since he acted like one. He sat there paused as if he couldn't believe this was happening. Like what was he thinking? I'd dump my boyfriend for him? He's clearly used to doing this, fucking wives and girlfriends and he clearly doesn't respect anyone but himself. He used me and I used him and it was wrong especially since I was trying to be mature. He then stood up then grabbed his clothes and started getting dressed.

"Whatever you bitch," he simply said.

I just rolled my eyes. I thought about saying something but didn't. He stayed silent but rushed to get his clothes on. Once he had done so he stormed out without word, thankfully. Once he had driven away I hit the shower and did the laundry to hide the evidence from my boyfriend. But you know as I thought about it that friend of his did me a favor. Our sex made me realize that I was unhappy with my boyfriend. I have a sexual hunger he just can't satisfy and I would always cheat on him whenever I could because of that.

Honestly I knew then that we were doomed as a couple but maybe we could be fuck buddies since I could teach him a few things, I do like being dominant in the bedroom. Even though his friend was an asshole he did me the biggest favor by making me realize I was denying who I was. And to think it only took some great sex to learn that. If only school had been like that, I would've been an honor student.

So make of that what you will Stiletto Desires but if you're wondering we did break up but became fuck buddies for almost a year. It was kind of weird but later on, after everything including the fuck buddy stuff, his new wife thanked me for teaching him some much needed sex skills. She assured me they were much appreciated on the honeymoon. Honestly I kinda wish I could join them sometime, see how he's been using those skills for myself.

Take care Stiletto Desires,

Insatiable

You take care as well Insatiable. That was quite a story, proves some men are really only good for one thing. But let's be fair sirens and remember that's not all men, there are some good ones out there. As for you Insatiable I have no doubt you have other saucy tales and I would love to hear them. When you do join your ex and his wife be sure to let us know, we'll be very appreciative of such a tale.

So dear sirens there you have it, proof that sex can give the answer you're looking for even if you don't know the question.

But let me ask you if you've ever had experienced something similar?

Ever desired one of the friends of the one you're with?

Ever caved into that desire?

Don't worry dear sirens, whether you did or not I don't judge. I only want your hungers fulfilled and with that turn the page for the next main course.

Hope you're hungry.

Heartbreaker

Dear Stiletto Desires,

My story is one that, if I'm to be honest, still confuses me. I'm not sure how to explain it but then I guess that means I should just tell you. Maybe telling you will help me figure it all out, just don't judge.

It goes back to last year when I first started college. I had the option of staying with my parents but decided to rent out a dorm room. I just wanted to feel independent and I thought being in a dorm would help with that. Anyway things were going well I guess, I mean I was doing well in my classes and making some friends and enjoying the odd party when my studies allowed for it.

My roommate was someone nice and fun, which was great we got along quite well. She wasn't as dedicated to her studies as I was so she would always poke fun and pester me to join her at one party or another. I had to turn her down a lot because I really wanted to get good grades so maybe the big firms would notice me and to make my parents proud. Okay maybe I was being too absorbed in my studies but I still made time for fun.

Well it wasn't long before my roommate had come back to our room with another girl. I was up for some gabbing and ice cream or heading out for some dancing or something and I thought that's what my roommate had in mind. Turns out she pulled me aside and asked me to leave so she and this girl could you know. Honestly I was taken aback, I mean I never met a lesbian before and I suddenly had a lot of questions and misgivings.

I know that's a terrible thing to say but I mean a lot of guys look at me in a certain way so wouldn't lesbians too?

If so would they try to force themselves on me?

Since my roommate was a lesbian has she been peeping on me?

Why hasn't she tried to hit on me?

Am I not pretty enough for her?

I didn't know what to think and I thought I'd do as she wanted and leave so I'd have time to think about all this. In the end I came up with nothing and wasn't able to study. The next few days came and went and because of my confusion I kept wondering if my roommate was going to try something while I was sleeping or in the shower. I didn't talk to anyone about it because I mean you get banned for less so I kept quiet fearing I'd get punished. But as it turned out I didn't have to keep things to myself as one night, a Friday, my roommate decided to interrupt my studying.

"Alright, so what the fuck is going on with you? You got a problem with me?" she asked.

I was flabbergasted, I had no idea she was mad at me and I didn't know why.

"No, why do you ask?" I answered hoping she didn't hear how nervous I was.

"Ever since I kicked you out of our room the other night you've been acting all weird around me. Are you pissed off about that? You should've said something because now I'm pissed at you," she revealed.

Suddenly I realized with all my confusion I was probably being terrible to her. I didn't mean to it's just I didn't know what to think and I'm not allowed to talk about it so what was I to do? I knew then I had to come clean because if I tried to lie about it that would only make things worse. I really hoped she wouldn't get angry with me for having my questions.

"Sorry it's just... look promise not to get mad?" I broached.

"No, I don't promise but it's because I'm a lesbian isn't it? That's why you've been eyeballing me and avoiding me?" she practically spat.

The venom was thick in her tone but I also heard some hurt and it made me feel bad.

"You have to understand, I've never met a lesbian before. Guys can be rather too forward and perverted and I was worried... well...," I confessed.

She looked at me for a moment as if reading the sincerity in my eyes. I noticed then she had really pretty green eyes and I could see how the other lesbians could fall for them. Her face softened and her anger seemed to melt away.

"So that's what this is about. You're afraid," she said.

She then walked over to my bed and sat down. She patted the spot next to her inviting me to sit down and I did. Her perfume was a bit strong but nice and as I looked at her I had to admit I was a little jealous of how pretty she was. Her lips were full and her breasts were bigger but not by much, still kinda hits the self-esteem though.

"Look, yea we lesbians can be as perverted and forward as men but we can also be respectful. It's why I never tried anything with you. Like don't get me wrong, you're hot in that nerdy girl way just you're my roommate and I had no idea how you'd react," she confessed.

I have to admit I never expected this. She was as much afraid of me as I was of her. Suddenly I felt completely relieved especially knowing we were both just misunderstanding each other. We probably should've talked sooner but I mean in this day and age of hypersensitivity and punishment why would we? I looked at her and smiled.

"So you're afraid too. We should've talked sooner, probably could've avoided all this," I offered.

She looked at me and I saw vulnerability in her eyes. She was pretty but seeing that vulnerability made her prettier and I had to admit her smile was lovely. Yea, I could definitely see why other women would want to sleep with her.

"Yea we should've. But look you don't have to worry about me, I would never try anything with you unless you wanted me to. Are you a lesbian?" she asked.

Suddenly my head was swimming, this whole thing was a lot. I mean finding out this was all a misunderstanding and we were both afraid. On top of that I was wondering why she never hit on me and here she was looking to see if she could. I mean I'd be lying if I said I wasn't flattered.

"I don't think so, I mean I've never thought about it so I don't really know," I confessed.

It was an honest answer and in hindsight maybe I should've lied. But you'll understand why when I tell you what happened next.

"Oh really? Maybe I can help you figure it out," she cooed.

I looked in her eyes and they turned to lust. I felt her place her hand on my thigh and I regretted wearing a skirt that day. But at the same time I got a little wet and I was curious.

"Maybe, I could do worse, you are pretty," I admitted.

She leaned in so close and I began to shake, this was happening and I did not know how to deal with it. I never had a boyfriend or girlfriend for that matter and not really used to these kinds of things. My mom was one of those tiger moms so she made sure I never had time for such things. She's Japanese and

I've heard that's normal in that culture. I must've seem stupid just sitting there wide-eyed and shaking, I worried she was going to laugh at me.

"Aw, you're shaking. You really never have been with a woman before. That's cute, you're cute. Let me help you," she softly said.

I felt her hand slowly slide up and I felt myself get wetter. I was soaking my panties and as I was reeling about the reality of this she then closed her eyes and kissed me. It's embarrassing but I squeaked a moan I didn't intend to, it just came out. I felt her tongue come into my mouth and I froze, I didn't know what to do. She pulled out her tongue and leaned back opening her eyes and looking into mine. When I felt her hand reach my pussy I jumped and screamed.

"Sh, it's okay. I'm sorry I'm going too fast, I'll take it easy and make sure you enjoy this," she softly said.

That made me feel better and more wanting this. I found myself calming down and just wanting to kiss her and did not move her hand away from my pussy. Instead I leaned in and kissed her and clumsily grabbed her breast. She pulled back and giggled then grabbed my hand and guided it to better grab her breast.

"Like this," she gently whispered, "The secret is not to try but to do what feels natural, don't think about it."

I nodded rather stiffly and did my best to surrender to my lust and desire as she instructed. We kissed again and this time I shoved my tongue into her mouth as she did with me. I let my tongue dictate what to do and found it rolling around her tongue and we tasted each other. As we kissed I started to gently squeeze her breast and she moaned when I did. I felt her hand slowly slide under my panties and onto my pussy. This time it wasn't a shock and I didn't scream.

I felt her fingers slide down to feel my entire pussy then pull back with her middle finger dipping ever so slightly between my lips. Once she had her fingers near my clit she stopped her hand and started to massage my clit in a circular pattern. I stopped kissing, unable to as I found myself breathing heavily and needing to moan. We stared deep into each other's eyes and though part of me thought this encounter was weird I ignored it so drowned in lust I now was. I shifted my position and had my legs spread, I was so wet and aching I wanted her on me. But I still afraid and I needed her to know.

"It's just not women I've not been with," I sputtered out.

God I was so afraid to confess that. How would she respond? Would she laugh at me? I hoped not and instead she broadened her smiled and she also adjusted her position so she too was facing me but she also moved closer and sitting between my legs.

"I'm glad you told me and I feel honored to be your first. I meant it when I said I'll take it easy and make sure you enjoy this," she assured me.

I'll admit I felt a bit torn. On the one hand she was a woman and that made this feel weird. On the other I was glad she was concerned with how I felt and was dedicated to ensure I would not be hurt. I had to kiss her again so I did and as our tongues entwined again I grabbed at her shirt and started pulling it up. She then pulled back, her smile still on her face and grabbed her shirt from me and took off her shirt for me. It was then I noticed she was not wearing a bra and her nipples were erect. I looked in her eyes and she nodded that comforting smile silently assuring me.

I bent down and brought one of her nipples into my mouth and I started sucking. She moaned and held my head and that made me want to nibble her nipple so I did. She gasped and moaned then moved her hands down my back where she grabbed at the bottom of my own sweater. I moved to her other breast and started licking that nipple. I felt my sweater being raised and felt it moved up past my bra. I paused to sit up and raised my arms so she could fully take my sweater off. Once she had dropped my sweater on the floor she reached behind my back to undo my bra.

I felt the bra loose and my breasts fall out of the cups. I started to shiver again and swallowed hard as she removed my bra and looked at my now freed breasts. She looked back up into my eyes and smiled that reassuring smile of hers and I felt myself starting to love it. It was just so comforting and made me feel that right here, right now was right and made me feel I could always be safe with her.

"Exquisite," she simply said.

She then bent low and with one hand she grabbed one of my breasts and with her other hand she grabbed my panties and started to pull down. Her mouth found its way onto my other breast and I tingled as she flicked my nipple with her tongue before she started to massage it. I needed to lie down and did and she moved to in response so she was on top of me. I felt as scared as I was turned on, I imagined my wetness was far more messy than it really was. She took a few seconds to suck my nipple then take as large and gentle nibble of my breast as she could. Once she had done that she kissed my chest between my breasts then kissed me lower on my stomach then again down on my waist before finally she was at my pussy and kissed my clit.

The sensations that sent through my body I can't describe, I never felt anything like it. But it became much more when I felt her teeth gently nibble on my clit. I raised my knees and tried to wrap them around her but I accidentally hit her too hard and bumped her head off my pussy. I looked up mortified I had done that and she just looked at me smiling yet again.

"It's okay, it's your first time, you're doing excellent and I can't wait for you to taste and touch me," she soothed gently.

I felt relieved then relaxed and kept my legs raised but not around her. She went back to my clit and started to lick and suck it. Things started to blur a bit and I wasn't sure when she was sucking and when she was licking. But it didn't matter, it felt so good and I didn't want it to stop. That's when I felt her fingers enter me. I gasped and moaned as she slowly slid them in never once did she stop eating my clit. I never expected to feel this much ecstasy but I'm so glad I decided to indulge in my curiosity and lust.

Slowly her fingers entered and slowly they came out until only the tips were in. Again and again she did this slowly building up speed and each time she pushed them in I would moan. Her fingers must've been so wet and I wondered if my own fingers would be just as wet when I was on her. Her fingers picked up speed and she pushed faster and faster. I moaned louder and louder and just as I wanted her to keep going and push harder she stopped and raised her herself to lie fully on top of me so I could stare in her eyes, her beautiful green eyes. We kissed again but she kept her fingers inside me slowly pushing in and out as much as she could.

"Join me, use two fingers," she instructed.

I kissed her and tasted her tongue and my own wetness. It was a taste I never thought I'd come to know but I greedily took her tongue and allowed it to get everywhere inside my mouth. As she instructed I moved my hands down to her waist and grabbed her shorts. I pulled them down as far as I could and felt around for her panties. Turns out she was wearing a G-string and I shoved those down as far as I could. I then felt around her shaved pussy until I found her hole and pushed two of my fingers in. She gasped and moaned and I tried to mimic what she was doing to me.

I slowly pushed my fingers in then pulled them out. At least I tried to. I ended up going as fast and as hard as I could. I just wanted inside her, I wanted to hear her moan as she was in me, as I was moaning in response. If she objected she did not say instead we stopped kissing unable to because of we were both moaning and gasping, breathing heavily when we weren't. We stared into each other's eyes as we continued to push our fingers into each other. My toes curled and I wanted more. I think she could sense this or see it in my eyes because then she stopped and gently placed her free hand on my chest.

"Have you heard of scissoring? Do you know what it is?" she asked me.

I had but didn't want to simply say it like that. Instead I thought I'd try to be sexy in answering.

"Don't ask me, just show me," I invited her.

Her face lit up and that made me smile. She adjusted herself so our legs we were between each other's spread legs. She then moved up until our pussies were against each other. It felt almost surreal, I never expected things to ever be like this. And to feel her pussy against mine, it was just wow, I don't know how to explain it I was already in sensory overload. Then she started grinding keeping herself propped up on her arm so we could stare into each other's eyes while we did this.

"Grind with me, it'll be better," she added.

I did, I imagined I was rather clumsy at it never having done it before but again if she objected she didn't say. But it felt so good, feeling her pussy rubbing against mine, our clits being rubbed against each other's body. We started to gyrate slowly at first but quickly I couldn't help myself and began to speed up. She sped up with me and we kept staring into each other's eyes and smiling. Faster we gyrated, it was like our bodies were becoming one and moving as one. I felt something build up in me but wasn't sure what it was.

"Something's happening," I stupidly and breathlessly sputtered out.

I started gyrating even faster and she kept up.

"Don't fight it, let it happen, you're going to love it," she said.

I did as she said and gave into this… whatever it was. I moaned louder and louder and soon as I gyrating as fast and as hard as I could. She moaned too and continued to keep up, our pussies rubbing and sharing their wetness. Finally I felt overwhelmed and stopped moving because I started shaking and my pussy spasming. It was too much and I screamed, our neighbors could probably hear me I was so loud.

If I was in my right mind I would've blushed deep red from how embarrassed I would've been from that. It wasn't until my body calmed down was when I noticed she had stopped gyrating as well but kept her pussy against me. Exhausted I collapsed and could only stare at the bunk bed above me. My roommate then disentangled herself from me and climbed up to lie next to me. I turned my head and kissed her again but this time just a peck, I only wanted to feel those soft lips of hers. She then wrapped her arms around me and sported that comforting smile of hers.

"That was an orgasm and I'm glad I could give it to you. Go ahead and rest, fall asleep if you want. I'm going to lie here next to you and just hold you," she told me.

I'm glad she did, this was all so much and I didn't know what to think. I closed my eyes but I wasn't sleepy. Honestly that surprised me because I felt exhausted. My roommate then snuggled up to me and true to her word simply held me. She kissed my cheek then laid still, her breasts and naked body pressed against me. I don't know how long I laid there but eventually I did fall asleep. When I awoke I looked over and saw she was still holding me and awake. She smiled and gave me a soft kiss on my lips.

"Morning," she greeted.

"Morning," I returned.

I suddenly felt awkward. All those feelings I suppressed last night of how uncomfortable it was to have sex with a woman came back. I knew then I wasn't gay and that this could only be a one-time thing.

"Sleep well?" she asked.

I paused to answer because I knew I had to tell her how I felt. I mean felt a lot closer to her but I couldn't date her or have sex with her again, it just didn't feel right.

"I did, but we should talk," I broached.

She briefly looked down and I could see sadness enter those green eyes. She then looked back up and while her comforting smile was there her sad eyes remained.

"No we shouldn't. I can see it in your eyes what you want to say. Do you regret what we did?" she asked.

I could see how vulnerable she was, she was exposed, raw. I knew regardless if I told her the truth or told her a lie she would get hurt. I hated being in that position, she didn't deserve to be hurt, not after what she did for me.

"No, I'll cherish it always and never forget. But we can't… well you know," I offered.

It was the truth but it still crushed her. I never knew she had feelings for me but I just couldn't be with her in that way. It wouldn't be fair for either of us.

"I know," she simply said, a defeated tone in her voice.

My heart broke. I really didn't want to hurt her but there was no way she wouldn't be.

"Are we okay?" I asked fearing the answer I knew was coming.

"No, I'll move to a new room," she said

I felt terrible but honestly I didn't understand why we couldn't go back to how things were.

"You don't have to do that, we can still be roommates," I offered.

She shook her head and I could see the tears she was fighting back start to form in her eyes.

"No, we can't. I always wanted you but I didn't realize how much I did until we did this. I want your heart but I know I can't have it, not ever. If we stayed roommates I would still try to get you. I would always try something and end up breaking both our hearts and we'd end up hating each other. I won't have that, not after this. I won't taint what we had even if it was a false promise," she said.

I didn't know what to say but I had to say something. I opened my mouth to tell her it wasn't a false promise but a wonderful and intimate moment between two friends that made them closer but she interrupted me.

"Don't, don't say a lie you want to believe," she told me.

I closed my mouth in reaction. I don't know how she read my mind but she was wrong, it wasn't a lie. I felt a lot closer to her and wanted her to stay in my life as a best friend. She stood up and got dressed and I watched her not knowing what to say or do. Once she was done she looked over to me.

"I'm going to stay somewhere else and I won't be back. I'll have someone come by to get my things. I know you think it'd be okay if I came back and got them myself but if I did I would only try to take you into my arms again," she told me.

I could see she was really struggling with this and her tears were still fighting to free themselves. She grabbed a few things, some books and her purse, then she walked to the door. Once she reached it I called out to her and she paused but did not look back at me.

"I will never forget this or what you did for me. But most importantly I will never forget you," I said to her.

I could feel my own tears start to stream down my face and part of me was glad she never turned around. She slightly raised her head and from the side I could see the tears finally loose themselves from the prison of her eyes. Without a word she left and closed the door behind her and I never saw her again.

To this day Stiletto Desires I look out the window or off in the distance wondering how she's doing. I kept my word and have never forgotten her or what she did for me.

And you know Stiletto Desires I know in my heart I never will.

Heartbreaker

Wow Miss Heartbreaker, that has to be one of the hottest and saddest stories I've ever heard. Unrequited love may be tough but what you had was still love, plutonic love is still love. So embrace those memories Heartbreaker and continue to cherish them. Always know whatever the future holds I'll be here waiting and listening if and when you're ready to share more. And never fear, I never judge.

So sultry sirens have you ever experienced unrequited love?

Is there a special someone you regret not pursuing or left behind?

Do you believe I would end this book with this tale?

Absolutely not, it's a great tale full of sexiness and sadness and love but I won't have you feeling sad when we're so close to the end. What kind of storyteller would I be if I did that?

So go refresh your drink and dry your eyes if needed and turn the page. I promise any tissues you need for this next confession won't be for your eyes.

One in a Million

Dear Stiletto Desires,

I'm not sure what story to tell you that could compete with what you may have. But I'm betting you've heard plenty of stories of lost loves or sex with assholes and that stuff. When my girlfriends and I talk sex those stories always come out so I imagine you get loads of the same. So hold onto your vibrator or whatever you use and sit back as I tell you the story of the guy I was not about to let get away.

So I started at a firm a few years ago. Things were fine the job was exactly as I expected, the money was decent and my coworkers, for the most part, were pretty friendly. It wasn't long before I hooked up with a small group and we would hang out together all the time. We'd often spend a Friday or Saturday night drinking and dancing or just hanging out at one of our places to watch movies and bullshit. It was really great.

After several months of getting used to my new and awesome routine the company was doing another round of hiring. There was no one who stood out except this one guy, really hot. He didn't look like he exercised but he wasn't fat either, right in the middle which I'll be honest sometimes I preferred in men.

Anyway I didn't do much of anything with this guy, I mean was happy with how things were and a relationship would put a kink in that. Not to mention dating a coworker? Not usually a good idea, never shit where you eat.

The company decided to assign this guy to the department I worked in. We ended up chatting and he was nice, not like so nice you keep in him in the friend zone though so the door was technically still open. As time went on he ended up joining our group and it turned out he had a good sense of humor. Suddenly I was wondering if maybe I should go after him. I was never one to wait for a guy to come after me, I'm the type of girl where if I see something I want one way or another I get it. Life's too short, waiting is how you miss out on opportunity. But I wasn't sure yet if I wanted to start something up with him.

A couple of weeks went by and I was coming around to deciding to date the guy. I mean he was funny, good looking but not the brightest bulb. We went to a couple of trivia nights and he'd get a lot of questions wrong, cost us a win at least once. But to be fair he was humble about it, owned it and we all ended up laughing over it. However he wasn't showing any interest in me.

No quick looks when he thought no one was looking. No fake excuses to be in the same room as me or to start up a conversation. No clumsy pick-up line in an effort to get my panties off. Nothing, just friendliness and the occasional joke. So being the girl who never waits I decided to I'd have to do the pursuing.

To this end I decided to spend a few days keeping an eye on him, to figure out his routine at work. I wasn't about to make excuses to keep him after the group went home after drinking. He was a good guy and definitely dating material and I didn't want to give the wrong idea. I didn't just want a fuck, I wanted more something real you know? And a night of drunken fucking is not you how start a lasting relationship.

Turns out every couple of day or two he would go into the supply closet to grab some office shit. Don't know what he as using all that for but it didn't matter, it was perfect. I could corner him and it'd be private, better than the break room or at his cubicle hoping not too many would overhear. On top of that it would help me provide… incentive to agree, make him an offer he couldn't refuse. If you catch my meaning.

So finally one day I worked up the courage and kept an eye on the supply closet. Like clockwork he inevitably walked to it and entered. I got up and quickly followed and paused to look around and make sure no one was noticing. I didn't think anyone was so I entered fast as I could just in case. I saw him reaching for some post-its, a few pens and couple of other things.

"Oh hey, can I reach you anything?" he asked when he saw me come in.

"Hi, just hold on," I simply said.

He looked confused by what I said but before anything else could be said I turned around and locked the door.

"What are you doing? You hiding from the boss or something?" he asked.

I stood up and slowly turned around. I was committed and he was not prepared for what I had in store for us. I imagine my lust was full in my eyes as I put on my seductive smile.

"Or something," I simply said flirtatiously.

I walked over to him and his confused face only deepened. His cluelessness on the situation was rather cute I had to admit and even turned me on even more. I was already wet and I could feel my hardened nipples being chaffed by my bra. So glad I wore my sexy red pair, a see through number with matching panties. I walked right up to him until I was pressed against him. I hoped he could feel my nipples poking him through our clothes but whether or not he could I felt his boner suddenly poke against me. I got even wetter, I wanted his cock more than anything right then.

"What are you doing?" he asked even as his breath quickened and his iris' widened.

It was so cute that even as turned on as he was getting he still didn't know what was going on. Oh this was going to be fun.

"Allow me to show you," I softly said as my own breathing was becoming heavier.

I kissed him, gently at first and laid my hands on his shoulders. After our kiss I pulled back and smiled again then looked deep in his eyes. They were blue, an amazing shade that weakened my knees. I was always a sucker for those eyes. He then smiled as he finally caught on and we kissed again. This time we reached out with our tongues and tasted each other. I gave a slight squeal as I felt his hands grab my ass and squeeze. I had not expected that. That made me giggle a little while we kissed which then caused him to giggle. I know we didn't have a lot of time unfortunately but I was going to have my fill and make sure he filled me.

I immediately slid my hands around his shoulders and down his back. I could feel he was on the sinewy side so at least he took care of himself, that bode well for what was to come. As I did this he would pull away on my ass and squeeze then pull me hard against him then pull me away again. It was a bit of a surprise, I didn't think he liked it that way. My own hands made their way to his ass and I took a quick squeeze. It was a great ass and I was thankful for that but I wanted the real prize, his hard throbbing cock.

Moving my hands around his hips I slid them to his crotch and grabbed his dick through his pants. He grunted and broke off kissing me to smile at me. I smiled back and resumed having my tongue taste his mouth and rub his tongue. He moved one hand up behind my back to crush me against him and oh how I wish we were naked because that would've felt so much better. Greedily I moved my hands up slightly so I could undo his belt and pants. Gravity dropped his pants and I loved the fact he was wearing boxers because now his boner was now free to poke me a lot harder. I lifted myself up so his dick would rub against clit when he finally freed it. God I was aching and hoped he understood we needed to do this before anyone came by.

I was rewarded because as we engaged in yet another kiss he moved his hands down to my skirt and undid it. My skirt dropped revealing my red see-through panties which were completely soaked by this point. I couldn't stand it and I wanted to have my way. So I grabbed him and turned him around causing us to end our kiss. I then pushed on him to get him on his back as I wanted to be on top, I'm always on top the first time.

He smiled and I just now noticed how sexy it was. It sent a thrill through me and I got down and yanked his boxers off. His dick flew up and quickly laid against him. I then stood back up and tore open my top. His eyes lit up when he saw my see through bra and I took a moment to revel in the ecstasy of that. Then I grabbed the front of my bra and undid it so my breasts would be free and his mouth opened so he could quickly lick his lips. This made me smile and I bent to down to take a quick lick of that hard throbbing cock of his. It drove him wild as he quickly closed his eyes and moaned.

I stood back up, quickly threw off my panties then straddled him. I paused again so he could see just how wet my pussy was. I wanted him to see the streams of my wetness I felt dripping down my legs and he looked and never blinked. I saw his cock throb in seeing all of me and his breathing got heavier. He was wanting me and letting me have my way. Oh how I love the cooperative ones.

I lowered myself and grabbed his cock. He gave a soft moan when I did and I could see it in his eyes the greed he had for my pussy. I wish we had more time because I would have teased his cock first but since we didn't I guided his dick to my cunt and lowered myself slowly until he was fully inside. We both moaned and I placed my hands on his chest. I started off grinding and he reached up to squeeze my tits. He did it gently and not rough which after my ass grabbing surprised me again. I smiled as best I could between moaning and grinding. I knew then this man would be an exciting fuck each time because he was able to surprise me so much while we fucked.

I then leaned down and arched my back so he could get his mouth on my tits. I started pounding his cock with my pussy and oh god it was hard not to scream. He grabbed one of my tits with his hand and pinched my nipple and I had to bite my hand to stifle my scream when he did. With his mouth he took as much of my breast into it as he could and gently bit down. He then moved most of his mouth off my tit keeping on my nipple in so he could suck it. During all this I kept pounding and pounding, and speeding up as much as I could. I wanted him to cum quick before we got interrupted.

He then moved his hands to my ass and squeezed as best he could, his mouth having then moved to my other tit so he could gently bite and suck. I ended up having to keep my hand in my mouth because I kept screaming from all the pounding of his dick I was doing. Soon, after a few more times I bounced on his throbbing cock he roughly grabbed my hips and held me still. He then started ramming me as fast and as hard as he could. He wanted to cum as much as I wanted him to. It did not take long as after several fast thrustings, and me fearing I would bite my damn hand in half, he finally rammed me as hard as he could and stopped, his dick fully in me and cumming.

I had to move my free hand to cover his mouth because he started to scream. As he came he pulled back once then rammed me hard again to finish shooting his load into me. Once he was done blasting his jizz I felt his grasp loosen and he lowered himself so he was lying flat on the floor. I looked down on him, I don't think he realized I wasn't done and had much more planned. He looked back at me and matched my smile. I got off him and he was going to try to get up but I grabbed his dick and started yanking it as it was already going soft.

"What are you doing? We could get caught," he breathlessly asked.

I smiled.

"I know but we're not done," I replied.

I then moved down still yanking and succeeding in getting him hard again. You have no idea how glad I was for that. I kept moving down his body until his now hypersensitive and newly hard dick was in my face. I took his dick and fully brought it into my mouth. I sucked and started bobbing my head up and down.

He moaned as I sucked and he gasped when I grabbed his balls and gently played with them. His moans heightened and I paused to look at him.

"Shhhh, could get caught remember?" I reminded him.

He breathlessly nodded and I grabbed his shaft. I gently pulled on it and stood up, he with me. I massaged his cock and turned him around so his back was to the rear wall. I then got on my knees and retook his cock in my mouth. I started moving my head back and forth fucking his cock with my mouth. He placed his hands on my head and let me continue to do what I wanted to his member. His hips started to gyrate slightly as I kept sucking and fucking. His dick was so hard and it was not long before I could feel him tremble from needing to cum again.

Suddenly he adjusted his hands to grab my head and stopped me. He then started ramming my face and I placed my hands on his thighs to brace myself. His balls smacked my chin as he fucked my mouth again and again. Never once did I stop sucking except when I needed to take a breath. He went faster and faster his moans were stifled as he bit his lip in an effort to keep his mouth closed. My own moans were muffled by his cock and suddenly I tasted the blast of cum he shot into my mouth. He slowed his fucking as he continued to cum and some of it blasted the back of my throat. Then finally he stopped and he loudly gasped and looked down at me. I continued sucking as I slowly removed my mouth so his dick was clean of everything but my spit and lipstick.

After swallowing his load, I mean since we were at work what else was I going to do with it, I looked up and smiled and he returned that smile. But that smile disappeared when I stood up and grabbed his dick again to start yanking again. I had heard guys could cum more than twice and saw it in a few porn. So I wanted to see if he could.

"More? I don't think I can, I think you killed my dick," he complained.

"If you're going to be with me you're going to have to get used to it," I told him.

He stayed quiet and just let me pull on his dick. Did I mention how much I love the cooperative ones? It took a bit but he did get hard again and that alone brought a look of pain on his face. I knew by that look he wouldn't last long and besides this was getting dangerous, someone could be trying the door any second now. That thought actually made me want this third time more, I mean the fear of getting caught is a real aphrodisiac. I kept yanking a little longer to ensure he was ready to fuck again. I then looked into his eyes.

"Your turn, just fuck me, pound my pussy like you mean it," I told him.

He smiled but the pain of his third hardened cock remained on his face. He pushed me to the floor and I resisted screaming from the shock of it. He got on top of me then grabbed my legs, spread them and pushed them upwards forcing my pussy directly upwards and right under his throbbing cock. He leaned in and positioned himself so his arms pinned my thighs next to my body. He then rammed his cock in me and I had to bite my other hand to keep from screaming.

It was amazing just how much stamina he had as he pounded me again and again. His cock going all in then almost pulling all the way out. I was so messy down there and it was all over him too. I raised my head so he could kiss me and he did. He never stopped pounding and pounding. With the position I was in his dick was hitting the right spot when he shoved it fully in and I could feel myself getting ready to cum. Faster and faster he went and he stopped kissing me as the pain of his hypersensitive cock ramming my sore and aching pussy was too much for him.

I bit my hand harder because I was screaming so much now. I felt my orgasm fast in coming and I hoped he would be able to hold onto his load until I did. Suddenly it happened, I widened my eyes and arched my back as I started to quiver from the orgasm I was now having. He leaned down and bit my shoulder hard as he started screaming from his own orgasm. As he shot his third load into me I sprayed all over him. In hindsight that was stupid, no doubt everyone would've at least smelled what we did considering how much of a mess we ended up leaving.

Once we both finished cumming we both collapsed and he slowly removed his obviously hurting dick from my pussy. I could feel it was already flaccid once he was out. He laid on top of me for a bit so exhausted he was and I liked that. It meant he was mine now and I liked how his body felt against mine. Once he had caught his breath he lifted his head to kiss me then got up and reached out his hand to help me up. I accepted and once I stood up I embraced him and kissed him one last time, ensuring my tongue would taste his so it would mix with the taste of his jizz and his cock.

"You should've brought condoms," he said once our kiss was done.

"With the men I pursue for a relationship I don't mind them cumming in me," I told him.

"So we're dating now?" he asked clearly surprised by my revealing this.

I bent down to grab my panties and his boxers. As we both put them back on I looked at him.

"Hey I don't fuck like this for just any guy. Didn't you notice how I was looking at you and laughing at your every joke this last week?" I confronted.

I bent down and grabbed his pants and tossed them to him then grabbed my skirt thankfully my top and undone bra were still on me I noticed.

"Well yea but I mean that could've meant anything. We were never alone and you never made a point of asking me to stay for one final drink or invited me to your place or whatever," he pointed out.

I smiled and gave a soft chuckle while I replaced my skirt. He was right, I never did anything more than look and subtly flirt, he could've easily have misunderstood my intentions. But I wasn't about to admit he was right, at least not until our relationship got serious. By this time he had already replaced his pants and had grabbed his shirt and was in the middle of putting it back on.

"Sure I could've done that but this seemed more fun or do you disagree?" I playfully toyed with him.

He paused and looked back over to me and smiled. Yea, I knew I was really going to fall in love with that smile especially with the way they made his beautiful blue eyes twinkle.

"Now don't be mean, that's not a good way to treat your new boyfriend," he challenged.

I smiled but had to suppress my delight. I wasn't about to let him know how sexy he seemed to me right then. I didn't know if our relationship was going to last but this was definitely a sign it was going to be fun. We both finished dressing then kissed again. We walked to the door and I listened for any sound of anyone nearby. If they were I didn't hear them. I then opened the door a crack and saw no one nearby then grabbed his hand and pulled him out with me. As we walked back to his cubicle I noticed he never let go of my hand. I was beaming, a good looking guy who was respectful and now showing he had a romantic streak? I hit the jackpot.

And to this day Stiletto Desires we're still together. We moved into a new place and learning to share the space. The fights haven't been too bad but always end in make-up sex. And my friends don't know but we've been flirting with the idea of marriage. Believe you me Stiletto Desires I have not and will not forget what a lucky woman I am for having him. And I make sure he never forgets how lucky he is for having me.

Thanks for listening,

One in a Million

Of the stories I've shared here that has got to be the hottest one Miss One in a Million. Thank you so much for sharing it with me and my sultry sirens. I can't speak for them but I'll admit I am in need of some serious cool down time. And congratulations on your relationship please do keep us in mind if you wish to share more of those tales. I will be listening and ready and aching for the undoubtedly dirty, dirty details.

So what'd you think sirens?

Was it too hot?

Was it not hot enough? You saucy minxes you.

But that dear sirens is the final story for you. Oh sure I could've provided more but, just like with sex partners, quantity does not equal quality. I do wonder which of these delicious and decadent stories was your favorite. Don't tell me, some mysteries are best left to the imagination.

Ultimately I hope you enjoyed yourselves, I know I did. Most importantly my sirens I hope your own scandalous escapades are as sexy and fun as you deserve them to be.

Stay insatiable and hungry my sultry sirens.

Finis